Dancing in the End-Zone

Bill C. Davis

A Samuel French Acting Edition

SAMUEL
FRENCH

FOUNDED 1830

SAMUELFRENCH.COM
SAMUELFRENCH-LONDON.CO.UK

www.SamuelFrench.com
www.SamuelFrench-London.co.uk

FOR PRODUCTION ENQUIRIES

UNITED STATES AND CANADA
Info@SamuelFrench.com
1-866-598-8449

UNITED KINGDOM AND EUROPE
Plays@SamuelFrench-London.co.uk
020-7255-4302

Each title is subject to availability from Samuel French, depending upon country of performance. Please be aware that *DANCING IN THE END-ZONE* may not be licensed by Samuel French in your territory. Professional and amateur producers should contact the nearest Samuel French office or licensing partner to verify availability.

MUSIC USE NOTE

IMPORTANT BILLING AND CREDIT REQUIREMENTS

DANCING IN THE END-ZONE had its Broadway premiere by Morton Gottlieb in association with Sally Sears at the Ritz Theatre on January 3 1985. The production was directed by Melvin Bernhardt, with sets by Douglas W. Schmidt, costumes by Patricia McGourty, and lighting by Dennis Parichy. The cast was as follows:

JAMES	Matt Salinger
MADELEINE	Pat Carroll
DICK	Laurence Luckinbill
JAN	Dorothy Lyman

DANCING IN THE END-ZONE was originally produced by special arrangement with Morton Gottlieb at Coconut Grove Playhouse on March 16, 1984 in Miami, FL. The production was directed by Stephen Hollis, with sets by David Trimble, costumes by Debbie Ann Thompson, and lighting by James Riley. The Production Stage Manager was Rafael V. Blanco. The cast was as follows:

JAMES	Frederic Lehne
MADELEINE	Elaine Stritch
COACH BIEHN	Tony Musante
JAN	Mary Joan Negro

Bill C. Davis was awarded a Drama-Logue Critics Award in 1990 for the Melrose Theatre production of *DANCING IN THE END-ZONE* in Los Angeles, CA. The Melrose Theatre production opened October 12, 1990 and was the first west-coast production for *DANCING IN THE END-ZONE.* The Director was Peter Sagal, with sets by Alexandra Rubinstein, lighting by Ken Booth, and costumes by KC Kelly and Shon LeBlanc. The Production Stage Manager was Ken Thompson. The cast was as follows:

JAMES	Scott Allyn
MADELEINE	Lois Nettleton
COACH BIEHN	Allan Feinstein
JAN	Käthe Mazur

CHARACTERS

JAMES BERNARD – the university's star quarterback
MADELEINE BERNARD – his mother
DICK BIEHN – his coach
JAN MORRISON – his tutor

AUTHOR'S NOTES

There are three playing areas:

I – James Bernard's furnished apartment –
Plush and impersonal

II – Jan Morrison's apartment –
An amusing amalgam of old and new.

III – The Locker Room, and the Meeting Room
for the University Board
of Directors, and Neutral area.

ACT 1

I (James' Apartment)

(JAMES *and* MADELEINE – MADELEINE *is and remains seated.*)

JAMES. Will you be all right if I go out for awhile?

MADELEINE. Jimmy – I told you before I came here, the only way this is going to work is if you just do whatever you'd do as if I weren't here. *(pause)* So where are you going?

JAMES. Coach Biehn's house.

MADELEINE. You spend a lot of time there.

JAMES. I'm going to help Andrea.

MADELEINE. That's *Mrs.* Coach – right?

JAMES. Right. We've got to get the leaves raked up around the house. They've got a lot of trees. Scott and Jeff said they want to help too. But they'll probably just jump into the piles.

MADELEINE. You're giving him a winning season. Do you have to rake his leaves too?

JAMES. I want to.

MADELEINE. *And* baby-sit his kids?

JAMES. It's really not baby-sitting.

MADELEINE. And what will Mr. Biehn do while you rake and they jump.

JAMES. He'll lie in the hammock with a scotch and soda, and watch.

MADELEINE. Ever the coach.

JAMES. It relaxes him. He has a lot of pressures. He can't wait to meet you.

MADELEINE. Why? Am I one of the pressures?

JAMES. No. You're my mother. He loves mothers. He asks about you all the time.

MADELEINE. It bothers him that I'm here, doesn't it?

JAMES. No. Not at all.

MADELEINE. Of course it does. A good coach is bothered by everything. What you eat – how much sleep you get; where you go at night; who you go home to. No wonder he loves mothers.

JAMES. So when should I tell him to come over?

MADELEINE. Jimmy – Do I need to meet him? I mean, you're not having any problems, are you?

JAMES. No.

MADELEINE. You're running less than you did last year, but…

JAMES. He expected that.

MADELEINE. And you more than make up for it with your arm.

JAMES. He says the same thing.

MADELEINE. And I saw your grades. Nothing less than a "B". I don't know when you do the work, but you're on the Dean's list. So you're golden. I don't need to meet Coach Biehn, and you don't need to rake his leaves. You work for him on the field – let him work for you *off* the field. He needs *you* Jimmy. Don't let him be so sure he has you. Keep him guessing. As far as he knows, a pro team could be trying to steal you away from him.

JAMES. I better get going.

MADELEINE. I'm only telling you for your own good.

JAMES. I know Mom. So you'll be okay for a few hours?

MADELEINE. *(smiling)* Jimmy. Just pretend I'm not here.

III (Locker Room)

BIEHN. Can you?

(*JAMES goes to him.*)

JAMES. It's going to be fine. I promise.

BIEHN. You don't need any distractions.

JAMES. She'll get better any day – really.

BIEHN. I've talked to the doctors here about her. You don't mind, do you?

JAMES. No. No.

BIEHN. They've checked her out – head to foot – and they're as confused as the doctors in your hometown. And how long has this been going on?

JAMES. Five months.

BIEHN. Is she going to need a shrink?

JAMES. No.

BIEHN. You really think you can help her? You move her two hundred miles and she's still in the same state. And we're coming into the toughest part of the season.

JAMES. She has to be with me.

BIEHN. You want me to talk to her?

JAMES. No – it's okay. Really. Don't worry. Please.

BIEHN. I just think it's too much for you Jaimie. Especially now that you have to get good grades on your own.

JAMES. What do you mean? Isn't that what I've *been* doing?

BIEHN. You don't read the school paper – do you?

JAMES. No. You told me not to.

BIEHN. Yeah. It's nothing new. Grades are a joke anyway. Some of the guys' grades were funnier than others. Christine's and Peggy's were hilarious.

JAMES. What about mine?

BIEHN. Yours were...cute.

JAMES. So I got a few gift-grades?

BIEHN. Don't worry about it. I know professors who give an automatic "D" to anyone who dangles a participle. It's a game. I just convinced some of the profs to play the game our way. *(pause)* Anyway – whoever got the scoop didn't put his name on the article, so I figured it wouldn't go too far. But then a couple of town papers picked it up, and then it hit UPI. What a mess. Never underestimate the anonymous donor.

JAMES. I don't know if that's right Coach.

BIEHN. I know. It shouldn't have even gotten in the *school* paper.

JAMES. No. I mean getting gift-grades at all. I don't know if that's right.

BIEHN. Oh come on. Don't you start on me Jaimie. The board of directors has been all over me about it. I hear enough from them.

JAMES. They're not going to fire you, are they?

BIEHN. They could. I broke the rules of the game. I got caught. It'd be fair

JAMES. If they fire you, I'll quit the team. I promise.

BIEHN. Don't get heroic Jaimie. As long as we win, I've got a job, and as long as you're on the team we're going to win. It's a simple equation. If you want to help, you can't fail anything.

JAMES. I won't. I promise.

BIEHN. Well – we're not taking any chances. You're going with a tutor.

JAMES. A tutor? No.

BIEHN. Yes. It's for your own good. And maybe we can talk her into doing some of the work for you.

JAMES. I can do the work myself. I don't need a tutor. *(pause)* It's a girl?

BIEHN. A *woman*. Get with it. She's older than the other ones – she's a graduate student – she has the best credentials, and she asked for you.

JAMES. Why?

BIEHN. Use your imagination. I've seen her at a few games. She watches you with binoculars. Can you believe it?

JAMES. Why?

BIEHN. I'm just going to warn you about one thing. You can flirt but don't fall in love. She's married.

JAMES. I don't believe in falling in love.

BIEHN. Oh. It that so? Why not?

JAMES. It's just a combination of overactive glands and being bored.

BIEHN. *(looking toward "I")* Very profound. Where did you hear that?

JAMES. It makes sense.

BIEHN. Maybe you're not bored, but at least give your glands a *chance* to get overactive.

JAMES. I'd rather put all my energy into playing.

BIEHN. I just don't want you blowing a gasket.

JAMES. My gaskets are fine. Honest.

BIEHN. How do you know? You never use them. *(pause)* That's funny.

JAMES. Yeah. So when do I see her?

BIEHN. Tomorrow.

JAMES. What's her name?

II (Jan's Apartment)

JAN. Jan Morrison. *(showing her credentials)* Here are the names and phone numbers of people I've tutored. Here are their grades before, and here are their grades after – feel free to call them.

JAMES. You don't need to do this. I'm sure you're fine.

JAN. How do you know?

JAMES. Coach Biehn said so.

JAN. I don't want you to take it on faith. We should go into this with confidence in each other.

JAMES. You have confidence in me?

JAN. Yes.

JAMES. How can you?

JAN. I've talked to your professors. I've read some of your papers and I've watched you play.

JAMES. With binoculars.

JAN. Yes. Now – you're taking Philosophy, Business Administration, English and – Dance? Why dance?

JAMES. The coach says it's good for my lateral movements.

JAN. Oh – that's interesting. And you don't have a major?

JAMES. Can't decide.

JAN. If you go professional, you won't *need* to decide, will you?

JAMES. No.

JAN. *Are* you going professional?

JAMES. If I'm asked.

JAN. I'm sure you will be. Maybe you should major in dance so you'll have something to fall back on in case you're not.

JAMES. *(laughs)* That's funny.

JAN. I bet you're a good dancer.

JAMES. Yeah – but have you ever seen a dancer sell shaving cream?

JAN. Is that what you want to do when you get out of college? Sell shaving cream?

JAMES. Is this part of the tutoring?

JAN. *(turns to his file)* Your main problem seems to be in philosophy

JAMES. Yeah – that doesn't come easy for me.

JAN. "Easily." "Philosophy doesn't come easily for me."

JAMES. Neither does English.

JAN. What's your problem in philosophy? Do you know?

JAMES. I don't like questions that don't have answers.

JAN. Questions in philosophy have answers…

JAMES. That are just other questions...

JAN. Which *are* answers. Some questions can't be answered. Some can. Let me ask you a question, and we'll see where it takes us.

JAMES. Okay.

JAN. Let me think. Well – let's get right to the point. Why do you play football?

JAMES. Why do I play football?

JAN. Yes. Why do you?

JAMES. I can't answer that.

JAN. Why not?

JAMES. That's like me asking you...

JAN. *"My"* asking you. That's like "*my*" asking you...

JAMES. That's like my asking you – "why did you get married?"

JAN. I can answer that. He said he wanted to make me happy every minute of the day. And I wanted to be happy every minute of the day. It was a perfect match.

JAMES. "Was?"

JAN. We're separated.

JAMES. I'm sorry. That's not easy, is it?

JAN. No. It's...well – it's somewhat like having a thousand pounds aim for your legs.

JAMES. What makes you think they aim?

JAN. Isn't that what they're supposed to do?

JAMES. *(pause)* No. Not at all.

JAN. Oh. But I read in a magazine that a player on the defensive line at MSU has fantasies about putting your knees in a blender.

JAMES. The defensive line of MSU wouldn't know a blender from a toaster.

JAN. All they really need to know is, which knee had the operation.

JAMES. How did *you* know...

JAN. I read the school paper. I'll bet they do too.

JAMES. *(pause)* Where were we?

JAN. We were looking for where a question would take us. *(pause)* You have a game tomorrow, don't you?

(**JAMES** *nods.*)

But the coach will make sure you get fixed up.

(**JAMES** *nods.*)

Tape?

JAMES. Yeah.

JAN. Ace Bandage?

JAMES. No.

JAN. Injection?

(**JAMES** *looks at her. He doesn't answer. He moves to III*)

III (Locker Room)

(**JAMES**' *leg buckles –* **BIEHN** *goes to him*)

BIEHN. Did it hurt all through the last quarter?

JAMES. No – no – it's fine.

BIEHN. You're releasing the ball too quickly, Jaimie.

JAMES. I know, I know. I'm sorry.

BIEHN. You can't let them intimidate you. They can smell it.

JAMES. We did win Coach. I'd never let us not win.

BIEHN. *(rubs* **JAMES**' *head)* I know. *(sees that he's soaked)* Hey Jaimie – why are you sweating so much?

JAMES. It's hot.

BIEHN. "Hot"? Today's high was 44. Two weeks ago it was 52, we played as tough a team, and you didn't sweat like this. You haven't been drinking. I mean – you don't drink.

JAMES. Just those two beers I had at your house.

BIEHN. I gave you beer?

JAMES. Yeah.

BIEHN. Oh. I was testing you. You weren't supposed to take them.

JAMES. Sorry.

BIEHN. Two beers should *not* make you sweat like this.

JAMES. I had a lot of fun with Scott and Jeff. They're great kids.

BIEHN. Yeah. We know. They're crazy about you too. That's old hat.

JAMES. Tell Scott that I put the picture of the horse he drew for me on our refrigerator door.

BIEHN. When you're worried, you sweat. What are you worried about?

JAMES. Nothing. Listen – I was thinking maybe next week I'd take Scott and Jeff to the zoo.

BIEHN. *(pause)* Okay.

JAMES. The fact is – *I* want to go to the zoo, and I need a couple of kids as a cover.

BIEHN. Okay. They'd love that. You should take Andie along too. She's an animal nut. She was the only psychology major who fell in love with all the experimental monkeys and rats. When she said she was in love with *me,* I didn't know how to take it.

(**JAMES** *laughs.*)

That's funny.

(silence)

It's your mother – isn't it? That's why you're sweating.

JAMES. No.

BIEHN. I'm going to talk to her.

JAMES. No Coach – it's okay. Really.

BIEHN. Jaimie – I know how to talk to mothers. I do it all the time. I live with one.

JAMES. I don't know.

BIEHN. You've been keeping us apart long enough. I want to meet her. *(pause)* She loves football?

JAMES. Ever since I started to play, she lives it.

BIEHN. Then she'll love me. Now hit the showers and don't sweat so much.

(**JAMES** *moves toward the showers, but stops.*)

JAMES. I think…I think…they're *aiming* for my knee

BIEHN. *(pause)* Let me tell you a little secret Jaimie. If they want to knock you out for the season, which they're dying to do, which you should take as a major compliment, that's what they're supposed to do. We'll fix you up a little better for the next game. *(Pause)* Don't worry.

(**BIEHN** *moves to I –* **JAMES** *moves to "II".*)

I (James' Apartment)

MADELEINE. Jimmy's all right, isn't he?

BIEHN. He's fine – he's perfect.

MADELEINE. Then why does he need a tutor?

BIEHN. Everyone on the team has to go with a tutor.

MADELEINE. No more gift-grades?

BIEHN. *(Pause)* Uh – no. Someone blew the whistle on that.

MADELEINE. Oh. Well – other than that – how is he doing?

BIEHN. On the field, he's doing great. His knee gives him a little trouble, but we manage. I'm sorry you and I haven't met sooner. There's a lot about Jimmy I want to tell you.

MADELEINE. Oh? I've missed something?

BIEHN. That's funny. No – I didn't mean it that way Mrs. Bernard.

MADELEINE. Good. Does Jimmy know you're here?

BIEHN. No. Absolutely not. This was totally my idea.

MADELEINE. "Totally." I see. Well tell me – are you as happy with Jimmy as you thought you'd be?

BIEHN. Definitely.

MADELEINE. He's good, isn't he?

BIEHN. "Good?" He's the best. I'll be honest with you though...

MADELEINE. Please.

BIEHN. When I first met him, I wasn't sure how he could survive on the field. But then I...

MADELEINE. I felt the same way when *I* first met him.

BIEHN. *(pause)* When he was born?

MADELEINE. *(pause)* Oh – he didn't tell you.

BIEHN. What?

MADELEINE. I adopted Jimmy.

BIEHN. *(pause)* No – he didn't tell me.

MADELEINE. Isn't that interesting?

BIEHN. Why didn't he tell me?

MADELEINE. Good question. Now there are some things about Jimmy that you wanted me to know?

BIEHN. *(pause)* Yes. Well – first of all – he's very concerned about you.

MADELEINE. "Concerned?" I don't like that word. It's weak. We love each other.

BIEHN. I know that.

MADELEINE. Then why are you trying to water down his love to a "concern?"

BIEHN. You're misinterpreting.

MADELEINE. No. I'm interpreting exactly right. You wish I weren't here.

BIEHN. Jimmy wants you here.

MADELEINE. I knew that *before* you came. Tell me something new.

BIEHN. All right. I've talked to your doctors here.

MADELEINE. *(pause)* Oh. The quack brigade?

BIEHN. The doctors here are the best. They operated on Jimmy's knee. And they say you can walk.

MADELEINE. Have they seen me walk?

BIEHN. Have they?

MADELEINE. No. So it's total hearsay.

BIEHN. They say you're *choosing* not to walk.

MADELEINE. People do that all the time. It keeps cab companies in business.

BIEHN. They think it's hysterical paralysis.

MADELEINE. Good for them. They found something to call it.

BIEHN. Is it?

MADELEINE. How would I know? I mean, can an hysteric know what makes her hysterical? Does she even *know* she's hysterical unless someone is good enough to tell her? Now ask yourself.

BIEHN. I have. And I think you know you can walk. You'd just rather not.

MADELEINE. Oh Coach Biehn – you think I'm that passive?

BIEHN. No. But I think what you're doing is an amazingly aggressive use of passivity.

MADELEINE. Jimmy told me your wife was a psychology major. That does have its share of benefits, doesn't it?

BIEHN. Yes. It helps me with my players. I'm more sensitive to their changes. Like Jimmy. He won't admit when something's bothering him – so he sweats. He went into that knee operation like a trooper – soaking wet.

II (Jan's Apartment)

JAMES. *(to* **JAN***)* Why did you ask me if I was getting injections?

JAN. You're sweating.

JAMES. No I'm not.

JAN. You are.

I (James' Apartment)

MADELEINE. You think *I'm* making him sweat.

BIEHN. I think he doesn't know what to do to help you.

MADELEINE. *(evading)* He doesn't need to help me. The college has sent me a wonderful big-boned girl – Lisa, which I thank you for. She's lots of fun, very strong and laughs at all my jokes. What more do I need?

(silence)

Jimmy insisted I come here. I didn't force myself on him. I don't force myself on anyone.

BIEHN. Then not walking must be awful for you.

(silence)

If you would just try to walk. I think if he knew that you were even trying, that would start to put him at ease.

MADELEINE. *(pause)* Mr. Biehn – let me be honest with *you* now. It's not good he's sweating. You're right to be concerned about it. But he's not sweating because of me. I promise. I'll find out what I can about it from this end. In the meantime, take the rake out of his hand, and you and your family take him out somewhere.

BIEHN. I'm sure we will, but…

MADELEINE. You know what he loves? Picnics. He hasn't been on one in so long. My husband never took him. We separated – my husband and I – and the next day Jimmy and I went on a picnic. He was so young and a little confused by all the packing and door-slamming. But we had a beautiful time that day. We had such a beautiful time, that when it was over, he said "Where is it?" I laughed and he got so mad, because he really wanted to know where that good time was. But he looked so funny. His hair was full of leaf-chips, he had acorns in his pockets and flower-petals in the cuffs of his pants. And I thought of a good answer to his question. Instead – I told him one of the trees captured the good time and it was trapped there. He said: "Which tree?" And I pointed to a big white birch. The next day, he was gone all afternoon. The police brought him home. His face was red and sweaty – he was drenched in sweat. His hands were blistered and cut from swinging the axe for so long. It wasn't our land, so he had no right to set the good time free. I had to pay a fine. But I didn't mind. It was the first time I saw how strong he could be. You should know – Jimmy is not a born football player. I knew if I could get him "swinging" he'd have a chance. That was his first step in basic training. I was a good coach too, Mr. Biehn.

II (Jan's Apartment)

JAN. You think he's a good coach, don't you?

JAMES. He is.

JAN. Well – Peter Farrell doesn't think so.

JAMES. Who's Peter Farrell?

JAN. He played here eight years ago, when Biehn first started coaching. He lost an eye during a grudge game. Did you know that's possible?

JAMES. It's happened.

JAN. Well, it happened here, and Farrell tried to sue the University.

JAMES. How could he sue the University? No one forced him to play.

JAN. He said Biehn authorized a shot of the painkiller, Toradol, before the game, which mixed badly with some medication he was taking and it affected his alertness.

JAMES. Did he get anything?

JAN. No.

JAMES. Were you here then?

JAN. No.

JAMES. Then how do you know about it?

JAN. Research.

JAMES. You've been "*researching*" Coach Biehn?

JAN. Yes.

JAMES. Why?

JAN. It started out as a class project, but then…

JAMES. Which class?

JAN. My major – Journalism. But then I found out some things that make Mr. Biehn very newsworthy.

JAMES. Newsworthy? He cares about his players; that's all that's newsworthy about him.

JAN. I heard he has girl names for all of you. Is that true?

JAMES. *(pause)* He's the best coach I could ask for.

JAN. What does he do that most other coaches don't do?

JAMES. A lot. He does a lot he doesn't have to do.

JAN. Does he authorize injections of Toradol for your knee?

JAMES. What if he did? I'm not saying he does, but what if he did. It wouldn't hurt anything. It'd just make it easier to get through a game. You think it's better to be in pain all through a game?

JAN. I think pain has a purpose. It lets you know when you're going too far or moving the wrong way. Sweating has a purpose too.

JAMES. *(pause)* Why did you ask to tutor me?

JAN. When I was watching you play, I got a very strong feeling that you really don't want to play.

JAMES. What? Are you kidding me? You're kidding – right?

JAN. No.

JAMES. You should clean your binoculars. *(pause)* We've won every game this season.

JAN. True.

JAMES. If I didn't *want* to play, do you think we'd be winning?

JAN. I think people who don't want to play are the fiercest players. When you're on the field you look like you're mad at yourself for playing.

JAMES. Mad at myself? For playing football? Now that's too much.

JAN. It must be.

JAMES. Well then why do I play, if it makes me so miserable?

(pause)

III (Locker Room)

BIEHN. Hey, Jaimie! Get over here!

JAMES. *(moving from II to III)* What is it Coach?

BIEHN. How do you feel?

JAMES. Good.

BIEHN. You up for the game?

JAMES. Yeah. Definitely.

BIEHN. How's the tutor?

JAMES. She's…she's smart.

BIEHN. Good. She's pretty too – huh?

JAMES. Different.

BIEHN. Did you make a pass?

JAMES. No.

BIEHN. I knew you wouldn't. Why did I even ask?

JAMES. How did things go with my mother?

BIEHN. Great, we're best friends.

JAMES. Thank God.

BIEHN. Hey – you free tomorrow?

JAMES. Yeah. Nothing planned.

BIEHN. What do you say we all go on a nice Sunday picnic somewhere? You know, take a hike, bring some sandwiches…just the family.

JAMES. *(hesitates)* Well…okay.

BIEHN. What's the matter? You don't want to?

JAMES. I'd like to get together very much. But I don't like picnics.

BIEHN. You don't? Oh. *(pause)* Well – then we'll do something else.

JAMES. What about the zoo?

BIEHN. Right – right. You were going to take Scott, Jeff, and Andie?

JAMES. Hey Coach – can I ask you something? Why don't you ever call Andrea, Andrea? Why do you call her Andie?

BIEHN. What the hell...

JAMES. I'm just curious.

BIEHN. Okay – I'll tell you. But don't tell anyone else.

JAMES. I won't.

BIEHN. Promise.

JAMES. I promise.

BIEHN. I can't stand any names that end with "A" – Like Anna, Lena, Tina, Melissa, Vanessa, or Andre-ah. Now, go suit up, then come see me.

JAMES. Uh – Coach. I was thinking – I know it's not good to be too confident, but I don't think we'll have much a problem winning this game.

BIEHN. You're right. It isn't good to be too confident. What are you getting at?

JAMES. I'd like to try this game with just the tape.

BIEHN. *(pause)* Why?

JAMES. I think it's good to know when it hurts. That way I'll know if I'm moving the right way.

BIEHN. If you move so it won't hurt, you'll get trampled – trust me.

JAMES. Could we just try it?

BIEHN. No.

I (James' Apartment)

JAMES. *(to* MADELEINE*)* Would you just try it?

MADELEINE. No.

JAMES. The muscles in your legs are going to atrophy.

MADELEINE. *(laughs)* Isn't that a funny word? "Atrophy". When you look at it on paper, it's spelled the same as "a trophy" – like winning "a trophy." I hope you win this year's MVP trophy. You could you know.

JAMES. Coach Biehn thinks so too. Isn't he a great guy?

MADELEINE. Well – he's… *(she stops)* Did you know he was coming here?

JAMES. Yes. Don't be mad at me. He's my best friend. You had to meet him sooner or later. Isn't he great?

MADELEINE. He's fine. He looks out for you. That's all I care about.

JAMES. What did you talk about?

MADELEINE. Well – first of all – he wanted to know why I wasn't walking. But I quickly shifted his attention to you, which wasn't difficult at all. You don't know it, but right now – you are the most important person in his life.

JAMES. No.

MADELEINE. Oh yes. But Jimmy – if he's such a great guy – why didn't you tell him you were adopted?

JAMES. You told him?

MADELEINE. It was the handiest diversion.

JAMES. Was he surprised?

MADELEINE. He was surprised *you* didn't tell him. It's important to him that you trust him.

JAMES. I do. I hope he doesn't think I don't.

MADELEINE. No – I'm sure he doesn't think that. After all, you trusted him enough to send him here to give me a "pep talk."

JAMES. I didn't "send" him. We just talked about it, and he thought maybe…we both thought…

MADELEINE. I don't mind. You told him I was crazy – I told him you're adopted, we're even.

JAMES. I didn't tell him you were crazy.

MADELEINE. It doesn't matter. I care as much about being crazy as you should care about being adopted. Why didn't you tell him? Were you afraid he wouldn't like you anymore?

JAMES. I wasn't not telling him on purpose. Was he mad?

MADELEINE. Don't worry about him. Let him worry about you. Which he does. Now – I want to know all about your tutor.

JAMES. *(pause)* Why?

MADELEINE. Well – she's a new thing in your life. Is she pretty?

JAMES. Coach Biehn thinks so.

MADELEINE. Married?

JAMES. Separated.

MADELEINE. *Married.* If she didn't say divorced – she's still married. What else?

JAMES. She asks a lot of questions. Like you.

MADELEINE. What kind of questions?

JAMES. She asked, "Why do you play football?" and "Do you want to sell shaving cream?"

MADELEINE. Oh – you'll be getting straight "A's" in no time. Why is she asking you questions like that?

JAMES. She's a journalism major; I guess, they're taught to ask a lot of questions.

MADELEINE. Oh – I see. I didn't know that. *(pause)* Coach Biehn said she *asked* to be your tutor.

JAMES. That's right.

MADELEINE. *And* she's pretty?

JAMES. Well – I don't know – Pretty's not the right word – I think most men would say she's sexy.

MADELEINE. What does her husband say? Where is her husband?

JAMES. I don't know. I don't even know if she knows. She married him because he said he wanted to make her happy every minute of the day.

MADELEINE. You're kidding. They're both lucky they're alive. How did you manage to find *that* out?

JAMES. She was trying to show me how simple philosophy is, and we sort of swapped questions. But I'm sure there's more to it than just what she told me.

MADELEINE. That's getting personal awfully fast. That's not like you.

JAMES. She's…provocative.

MADELEINE. "Sexy" "provocative" Are you sure she's not a stripper?

(**JAMES** *laughs.*)

I think we should get you a new tutor.

JAMES. Why?

MADELEINE. I don't think she's interested in your grades at all.

JAMES. What do you think she's interested in?

MADELEINE. Coach Biehn told me that the only reason you *need* a tutor is because someone went to the press with the news that you players were getting gift-grades. It sounds like the beginning of a wonderful class project for a journalism major.

II (Jan's Apartment)

JAN. It was not a class project.

JAMES. Then why did you do it?

JAN. I've got a better question. Why did you accept grades you knew you had no right to?

JAMES. I didn't know I was getting gift-grades.

JAN. They were forced on you?

JAMES. They slipped by me.

JAN. That's even worse. You thought you were doing good work, when in fact...

JAMES. Look – I'm not going to try to defend that. I can't. But I resent what you did. People love to hear that football players are either dumb or on steroids. You gave them just what they wanted.

JAN. *(pause)* Do they love to hear you're crippled?

JAMES. I'm not crippled.

JAN. You could be, if you keep playing with painkillers.

JAMES. *(pause)* Did you get paid for writing that article?

JAN. *(pause)* No.

JAMES. Has UPI promised you a job after you graduate?

JAN. *(pause)* UPI doesn't know I wrote it.

JAMES. What about your professors?

JAN. They don't know either. For class, I do articles about local candidates. You, and the editor of the school paper are the only ones who know I wrote that story.

JAMES. How do you know I won't tell everyone it was you?

JAN. I don't know. But I'm going to ask you not to.

I (James' Apartment)

*(***MADELEINE*** and ***BIEHN****)*

MADELEINE. You have to get him away from that woman.

BIEHN. *(pause – looking at her)* Which woman?

MADELEINE. The tutor.

BIEHN. Is that why you called me to get over here right away?

MADELEINE. Yes.

BIEHN. *Un*believable. I interrupted a defense scrimmage, because I thought you were ready to walk.

MADELEINE. She's a journalism major.

BIEHN. Yeah. I know. So what?

MADELEINE. I think she's the one who wrote the story about the gift-grades.

II (Jan's Apartment)

JAMES. *(to* **JAN***)* Were you afraid to take credit for it?

I (James' Apartment)

BIEHN. No way. She's a fan. I've read articles she's written. She writes about local candidates, and county fairs. She doesn't even write like the anonymous donor.

II (Jan's Apartment)

JAN. Credit's not important for me for that story… *(pause)* …or for the story I'm working on now.

I (James' Apartment)

MADELEINE. You don't understand. She asks him too many questions.

BIEHN. That's her job. That's what tutors do.

MADELEINE. She asks him why he plays football; or if he wants to sell shaving-cream when he grows up.

BIEHN. She's trying to break the ice. Look – now that I'm here; what do you say we try a few steps?

MADELEINE. Never mind about that. Listen to me. Jimmy can be very impressionable. He's loyal to you, but he's describing this woman as "sexy" and "provocative". Loyalty doesn't stand a chance against those two.

BIEHN. I'm not worried about Jimmy's loyalty. Anyone as punctual as Jimmy has to be loyal. He lives on Lombardi-time. You know what that is?

MADELEINE. Of course.

BIEHN. Okay smarty. What is it?

MADELEINE. It's ten minutes earlier than when you're supposed to be there. Do I pass?

BIEHN. Very good. And I'm not just talking about practice. When he visits – I say 7:30 – he's there at 7:20.

MADELEINE. I don't like it. I don't like the way he talks about her.

BIEHN. Mrs. Bernard – What's your first name?

MADELEINE. Madeleine.

BIEHN. Well – Madeleine – I have to ask you this. Does it bother you that he's interested in another woman?

MADELEINE. Too bad your wife didn't major in Home Economics. Then you'd only be dangerous in the kitchen.

BIEHN. Okay – fine. You won't help this situation by walking, but at least don't discourage him from liking this other woman. I'm glad he thinks she's sexy. I'm relieved. He needs a nice wholesome fling. Let him have it. You can't keep him forever.

MADELEINE. A "fling?" Mr. Biehn – what's *your* first name?

BIEHN. Dick.

MADELEINE. Not "Richard?"

BIEHN. Yuk.

MADELEINE. Alright – Dick. I have to tell you. If you have any plans for a winning season, there are some things about Jimmy *you* should know.

II (Jan's Apartment)

JAMES. What are you planning?

JAN. I have no bad intentions.

JAMES. You just have questions.

JAN. I just want to know…

JAMES. What?

I (James' Apartment)

MADELEINE. He was given up by both his fathers. The first time he was three – the second time he was nine. My husband rejected Jimmy every day; I watched it until I couldn't watch it anymore. I made my husband leave.

II (Jan's Apartment)

JAN. Does Coach Biehn really…

JAMES. I'll answer your questions about me, but you can't ask me anything about Coach Biehn.

JAN. All right.

I (James' Apartment)

MADELEINE. When Jimmy was ten, he would carry his best friend's books home for him. I had to tell him not to. When he was fifteen, he made a horrible fool of himself over a girl – Pattie Collins. After braving two parties together, Jimmy was sure it was love. She wasn't. She never knew what hit her. Letters, phone calls, gifts, tears. Poor Pattie Collins was completely confused. Jimmy was very good looking – even then. He didn't need to do all those things but he did – so he lost. And for a few years there, it became a pattern. The Pattie Collins' pattern. Sounds like a dress, doesn't it? But it was more like a fit. Once it was so bad he put his hand through a pane of glass.

II (Jan's Apartment)

JAN. Is it true you throw up before each game?

JAMES. Yes.

JAN. Why?

JAMES. The full-back, John Pagones, makes himself throw up before each game. He feels it makes him play better. And when *he* does it, I get kind of sympathetic reaction and then I throw up.

JAN. *(pause – looks at him)* Oh. Oh. *(pause)* What do you feel like when you suit-up?

JAMES. What do I feel like?

JAN. What goes through your mind?

JAMES. *(pause)* I...I go over the plays, that's all. What do you think of when *you* get dressed?

JAN. On warm days I think how nice it would be not to bother. You know – when you're all suited up, you look like a tank.

JAMES. Really? I feel more like a Rhino

JAN. Rhinos look like tanks.

JAMES. Yeah – I guess so.

JAN. When you took off your helmet, I was amazed at how attractive you are. Even with all that mascara on your cheekbones.

JAMES. It's not mascara.

JAN. What is it? Tar?

JAMES. *(laughs)* No.

JAN. War paint?

JAMES. *(smiling)* That's what Coach Biehn calls it.

JAN. I know. But we're not supposed to talk about Coach Biehn. *(pause)* Actually – there *are* those who think football *is* just like war.

JAMES. No. It's a game. It's strategy.

JAN. Isn't war strategy?

JAMES. Yes, but...

JAN. Isn't war armor, and helmets, and front lines and injuries *and* casualties – just like football?

JAMES. If everyone in the world suited up in a football uniform, there probably wouldn't *be* any more wars.

JAN. So you think football is a healthy ventilation – for the players *and* the crowd?

JAMES. What do *you* think?

JAN. I really should just ask the questions.

JAMES. No – you should talk to me – tell me what you think.

JAN. I think the way you play is the way you live. If you play war, you live war.

JAMES. No. You can't say that. You can't call football *war*. It's a dance; it's precision; it's comradery. Those thousands of people watching are just having fun. You don't *really* think that football is war?

JAN. It's penetration of territory – it's defense of territory. It's a way of thinking. It's a militaristic game of dominance. It has armor and helmets, like soldiers – and casualties – wounded and disabled. I think you and your comrades are treated like cannon fodder.

JAMES. You have to be the only person in the world who sees football like that.

JAN. I've written to some of the football alumni. The ones who coach Biehn took a special interest in; like he has with you.

JAMES. Oh – your research?

JAN. Yes. One player who said his best weapon was his head, had seven concussions. He wrote he's had a headache for five years – anger; confusion; no sleep. And then players with every other kind of injury – like yours – most of which were ignored and overed up by Biehn.

JAMES. Go ahead. Let me hear what they say.

Jan. You might not show up for our next lesson.

JAMES. You wouldn't care.

JAN. *(pause)* You're wrong. I would.

I (James' Apartment)

MADELEINE. I'm right about this Mr. Biehn. Listen to me. I know my son. I've never known anyone like him.

He touched everyone as if that touch made them his forever. At a certain age he had to stop being an open wound. Because that's really what he was – a fresh, red wound. Football was and football is the bandage. It had to be. He couldn't go through life touching people and letting people touch him the way Jimmy would. So I made sure he learned to touch according to the rules.

II (Jan's Apartment)

(JAN shows Jimmy a folder of letters.)

JAN. So far, I've gotten thirteen letters. One of them is from Peter Farrell. *(silence)* You want to know what they say?

(JAMES doesn't respond – JAN pulls out a letter.)

Paul Hoover – "I severely sprained my ankle on a Wednesday practice. So coach Biehn authorized an injection for the Saturday game. For the next month my ankle had to be injected before and during each game. *Now* I take a pint of painkillers with my morning coffee, just so I can get to work."

I (James' Apartment)

MADELEINE. I had to tell him to treat everyone the same. Show them that you can do without them; that you can let go and not feel a thing.

II (Jan's Apartment)

JAN. Martin Sanders – "I now have intolerable, chronic pain in my left leg from injuries that were misdiagnosed. One doctor now is suggesting I lose that leg. In fact at the time I had bone-chips. But Biehn never dealt with my complaints except with Toradol and painkillers which I pretended to take. I used to play with tears streaming down my face."

I (James' Apartment)

MADELEINE. I told him not to cry in front of people. They'll say they understand. But they'll be glad to see you weak. They'll pity you and want to stay away from you. Solitude should always be *your* decision.

II (Jan's Apartment)

JAMES. What are you going to do with those letters?

JAN. Take them to the school paper; get them printed, and maybe they'll go the same route as the story about the gift-grades.

JAMES. Why?

JAN. I just decided that this is my world too – and I'm making a claim for it. I want to show football for what it really is. It's war and war is the national sport – *(showing the letters)* This is a casualty list. And Coach Biehn, like everyone else at the top, doesn't care what the body count is, as long as he wins.

JAMES. Don't print those letters.

JAN. I have to.

JAMES. You'll ruin his life. I can't let you do that.

JAN. *(pause)* You're a good friend, Jimmy. I don't know why I'm surprised.

(She gets another stack of letters.)

JAN. Your first assignment. These are copies of all the letters. Take them home – read them, and then let's talk about ruined lives.

*(She offers the letters to him – **JAMES** doesn't take them.)*

(pause) I should tell you. There's another letter from an alum who was very angry with me. Chuck Reilly – he grew up right-handed, but now, because of a neck injury and a concussiond, he wrote this to me with his left hand. "Leave Coach Biehn alone. Whatever he expected from me I was willing and more than ready to give. No one made me play football. I was aware of all the risks and if I was given the chance to play under Coach Biehn again, and I knew I was going to *lose* my hand, I'd still play, without a second thought. Life after football has been all downhill." *(to JAMES)* Could you write a letter like Chuck Reilly's ten years from now?

(silence)

Would you write a letter like Paul Hoover's or Martin Sanders' now?

JAMES. That's why you asked to tutor me – isn't it?

JAN. Yes. I wanted a letter from you. I still want one. But whether you write a letter or not, I want you to wake up to what's being done to you. You walk around the field between plays like you're some kind of old warrior: hands on your hips and you've got this real "manly" swagger. On the field it's a swagger – in life it's a limp. And it's going to get worse. Through the binoculars – in principle – it bothered me. But now that I see you – up close… *(pause)* I can't stand the thought of anyone trying to hurt you.

I (James' Apartment)

MADELEINE. He had leaf chips in his hair, acorns in his pockets and flower petals in the cuffs of his pants. *But* I got him swinging – and he was safe. But now – listen to me Coach Biehn – either get him away from that woman, or start looking for a new quarterback.

II (Jan's Apartment)

(**JAN** *holds out the copies of the letters to Jimmy. After a pause, he takes them, and exits to "III".*)

III (Locker Room)

(**BIEHN** *holds a protective plastic mask to* **JAMES**)

BIEHN. What the hell was this doing in your locker?

JAMES. *(taking it)* Its for eye protection.

BIEHN. You don't need it.

JAMES. I've been reading, and… *(stops himself)*

BIEHN. What? *(pause)* What have you been reading?

JAMES. *(pause)* Just – reading. I mean – how else can I get "A's"?

BIEHN. Get "A's" but don't get paranoid. Now, give me that. It'll give you a headache.

JAMES. I get them anyway.

BIEHN. What's the matter with you Jaimie?

(**JAMES** *looks at* **BIEHN**, *then looks away. He puts on the mask.*)

BIEHN. Oh Christ – you look like a goddamn space-invader.

JAMES. I want…protection.

BIEHN. Are you saying the guys on the line don't protect you enough? You want me to tell them that?

JAMES. No. No. But – *(pause)* What about Peter Farrell?

BIEHN. *(pause)* Who told you about him?

JAMES. He lost an eye. Didn't he?

BIEHN. *(pause)* Now, that's it. I'm not taking this prima donna crap. Not from you, not from anyone. Now – take it off.

(**JAMES** *takes it off.*)

JAMES. Should I come in and see you after I suit-up?

BIEHN. No – play without it today.

(*He walks away* - **JAMES** *starts to move to* "*II*". **MADELEINE** *stops him.*)

I (James' Apartment)

MADELEINE. You lost.

JAMES. Hm – hmm.

MADELEINE. What did Coach Biehn have to say?

JAMES. Nothing. To me.

MADELEINE. Where are you going?

JAMES. To the tutor.

MADELEINE. How's it working out?

JAMES. Fine.

MADELEINE. What's she teaching you?

JAMES. How to think.

MADELEINE. Maybe that's why you lost.

JAMES. Mom? When did I go out for a football team – for the first time? I can't remember.

MADELEINE. (*pause*) Eighth grade. You should remember that.

JAMES. Why?

MADELEINE. Because you didn't make it.

JAMES. And when did I try out again?

MADELEINE. Tenth grade. And you went straight to Varsity. You have to remember that.

JAMES. But whose idea was it?

MADELEINE. Jimmy…

JAMES. I just can't remember if I said: "Let me play", or "Let me try out", or if you said…

MADELEINE. Jimmy. You're a football player. Period.

JAMES. I just want to know how it happened.

MADELEINE. I see. First – *when.* Then – *how.* And pretty soon you'll be able to answer the tutor's questions – "Why?" Then who knows what'll happen.

JAMES. *(pause)* I don't want to be late.

(**JAMES** *goes to* **JAN.**)

II (Jan's Apartment)

JAN. You're ten minutes early. *(pause)* I wasn't even sure you were coming.

JAMES. Listen – I want to keep those letters you gave me. I read them all – twelve times. I can't talk about it yet.

JAN. All right.

JAMES. Please don't print them. Please.

JAN. *(pause)* How's the knee?

JAMES. It's fine.

JAN. Really?

JAMES. No – it hurts.

JAN. Did it hurt during the game?

JAMES. Hm-hmm.

JAN. You played without it?

JAMES. Hm-hmm

JAN. You think that's why you lost?

JAMES. I don't know. The team is certain we lost because I didn't throw up.

JAN. You didn't?

JAMES. First game this season I didn't. I think Pagones was kind of hurt too. *(pause)* So what are we learning today?

JAN. German Philosophers. They're the toughest. You should have brought your helmet.

JAMES. What's your husband's name?

JAN. *(pause)* Rich.

JAMES. As in Richard?

JAN. Yes.

JAMES. That's Coach Biehn's name, except his friends call him "Dick."

JAN. I wonder why.

JAMES. You shouldn't be so hard on him.

JAN. Sorry.

JAMES. He is my best friend.

JAN. But why do you always call him "Coach Biehn?"

JAMES. He wants it that way. I understand that. I have to be the same as every other player.

JAN. Are you?

JAMES. *(pause)* He's a good guy – really. You know, once a month he volunteers a free day to drive kids with cancer to the Marion Clinic.

JAN. That's very nice of him. He could be a saint for all he knows. But I can't forget the letters.

JAMES. Couldn't you just show the letters to the board of directors? They'll give him a warning. But don't print them. It'll kill him – I know it.

JAN. *(pause)* Let's get down to business

JAMES. What does Rich do?

JAN. That's not business.

JAMES. But I want to know about you.

JAN. He's a lawyer. A public defender. The first German philosopher we're going to…

JAMES. Where is Rich now?

JAN. He's in prison.

JAMES. Are you kidding me? Your husband's in jail?

JAN. *(laughing)* This isn't Dodge City, Jimmy. He's not in "jail". He's in prison.

JAMES. But what for?

JAN. Tax evasion

JAMES. He made a mistake?

JAN. No. He did it on purpose. He figured out the percentage of his taxes that paid for the military, and he refused to pay that amount.

JAMES. Did he tell you he was going to do that?

JAN. He did – and I told him I don't think it's going to help. Bombs exist. Plans for bombs exist. You could defuse all of them tomorrow, but sooner or later they'll come back. *We're* the ones that have to be defused.

JAMES. Was that why you and he separated? Because he got arrested?

JAN. No – we separated a month before that.

JAMES. Why?

JAN. *(pause)* He wanted children. I didn't.

JAMES. What are you going to do about him? Are you going to divorce him?

JAN. I don't know. I have a few things to figure out.

JAMES. Could he divorce you in the meantime?

JAN. He could.

JAMES. Would that upset you?

JAN. I haven't thought about it.

JAMES. Do you still like him?

JAN. Of course.

JAMES. What do you like about him?

JAN. I like that he's willing to risk bringing children in to the world.

JAMES. And you're not?

JAN. No.

JAMES. *(pause – slowly)* I think *you* having…I mean – *your* having children would do more good than going to prison, or quitting the team, or anything anyone could do.

(JAN *touches his face.*)

III (Locker Room)

BIEHN. What the hell was that all about Jimmy? That was the worst first half I've ever seen you play.

JAMES. Sorry – I...

BIEHN. Sorry's no good. What are you thinking about out there?

JAMES. Nothing...

BIEHN. Well start thinking about winning...

JAMES. Yes, sir.

BIEHN. Cause we're losing – do you know that?

JAMES. Yes, sir.

BIEHN. Have you bothered to check the scoreboard? If we lose, it'll be totally because of you. Just know that.

II (Jan's Apartment)

JAN. What *were* you thinking about out there?

JAMES. *(pause)* You.

JAN. Oh.

JAMES. We lost – again.

JAN. Are you all right?

JAMES. Yes. Because this time I didn't care. Somehow that felt better than any touchdown ever. We lost – and I didn't care.

(**JAMES** *kisses her. It lasts for awhile,* **JAN** *gently ends it.*)

I (James' Apartment)

BIEHN. *(to* **MADELEINE***)* Okay – you win. Now we're tied for first place. Does he know how important this season is? I mean, this could make him for life. He could make enough money in the next few years so that neither one of you would ever have to walk again.

MADELEINE. That sounds like fun.

(silence)

BIEHN. It's the tutor – like you said – isn't it?

MADELEINE. You should have listened to me, Mr. Biehn. You dismissed me as being crazy much too soon. You should have waited. I would have given you other evidence for that. But I am stunningly sane when it comes to knowing the enemy.

III (Neutral Ground)

(JAMES and JAN are on a picnic. They're drinking wine.)

JAMES. ...and she pointed to the biggest white birch I'd ever seen, and she said – "There – that tree captured it. It's trapped inside that tree."

JAN. And what did you do?

JAMES. I tried to chop it down – for six hours – until my hands started to bleed.

JAN. Is that why you stopped? Because of your hands?

JAMES. No – A trooper stopped me.

JAN. Oh – it wasn't your tree?

JAMES. No. It belonged to the State. *(pause)* It took forever for my hands to heal. *(showing his hands to her)* You can still see a few dark spots. I guess that's how the palms of your hands heal.

(She holds his hands as she looks at them. Silence.)

Can I ask you a question?

JAN. That's the only question you *haven't* asked me.

JAMES. Why don't you ever call Rich?

JAN. *(pause)* I don't think he has a phone in his cell.

JAMES. You could get in touch with him somehow.

JAN. I suppose I could.

JAMES. So why don't you?

JAN. He told me *not* to call him until I was ready to start a family.

JAMES. Oh. *(pause)* Can I say what I think?

JAN. Alright.

JAMES. I think you do want to have children. I think that's why you're trying to…change the world. But you can't change the world – it's just the way it is.

(Silence – she drinks her wine – he drinks his.)

JAN. You have a game tomorrow.

JAMES. *(as he drinks more wine)* Hmm-hm.

JAN. Should you be drinking?

JAMES. No. No wonder Coach Biehn doesn't want you to be my tutor anymore.

JAN. He said that?

JAMES. Yeah. But I told him I wouldn't switch. It was the first time I stood up to him. It scared me a little. He said he wanted to talk to you.

JAN. Really.

JAMES. He could come over – couldn't he?

JAN. *(pause)* Well…

JAMES. The three of us could get along, you know. We could.

JAN. Are you playing without it tomorrow?

JAMES. Don't know.

JAN. *(pause)* I worry about you.

JAMES. Sometimes, I think you're the only one who does.

JAN. Doesn't your mother worry about you?

JAMES. Not when it comes to football, she doesn't.

JAN. She must.

JAMES. She never tells me she worries. She never came to the hospital when I had the operation.

JAN. Why not?

JAMES. I'm not sure. I thought she would, but to her, it was almost like I didn't *have* an operation. *(pause)*

JAMES. *(cont.)* Maybe she didn't want to make a big deal about it. It's important to her that I keep playing.

JAN. But Jimmy – what's important to you?

> *(pause)*

> Do *you* want to keep playing? You know what everyone else wants you to do; – what do you want?

> *(silence)*

> Jimmy?

I (James' Apartment)

MADELEINE. Jimmy – no.

JAMES. *(going to her)* Listen to me…

MADELEINE. You don't want to quit. You're doing it to impress her.

JAMES. I don't need to impress her.

MADELEINE. You're setting yourself up. She only looks for interesting conquests.

JAMES. You don't know her.

MADELEINE. She'll brag to her friends – "I made him quit."

JAMES. Mom – it is *my* decision

MADELEINE. You're giving yourself up to her completely – unprotected. And when *you* stop caring about protection, I get scared.

JAMES. Don't be scared. I'm not.

MADELEINE. You don't remember how I found you.

JAMES. *(laughs)* I was a baby.

MADELEINE. You were four. Four is not a baby. They couldn't keep you out of corners. That's where I first saw you – huddling in a corner. Your tutor looks for a peak only so she can stick her flag into it. Then she'll move on, and the peak becomes a corner very quickly. I don't want to see you there again.

JAMES. Mom – I *am* in a corner. I carry it around with me. I'm suited up all day. I don't want to be anymore. I want someone to come to me, instead of coming *at* me. I don't want to learn to dance to get away from someone. I want to dance *with* someone.

III (Locker Room)

BIEHN. Jaimie – go suit-up.

(JAMES *moves to him.*)

JAMES. I…I can't.

BIEHN. (*pause*) What?

JAMES. I can't.

BIEHN. Can't what?

JAMES. I can't play anymore.

BIEHN. What?

(*silence*)

Jaimie. Stop fooling around. We're going up against a team that could knock us out of first place.

JAMES. I know that you care about that. But I don't anymore. I can't tell you why. I just don't care about first place anymore. And I want to tell you – face to face – because – you've been so good to me – and also to tell you that you should start thinking about quitting, too.

BIEHN. I should…quit?

JAMES. Yes, it may be your only way out.

(*silence*)

BIEHN. Look – why don't you and I go somewhere after the game? We'll have a couple of beers – just a couple. I know I haven't paid as much attention to you as I should…

JAMES. No – you've been great. You're my best friend. I'm probably not *your* best friend…

BIEHN. Jaimie – for Chrissake…

JAMES. But I hope you at least think of me as a friend.

BIEHN. Of course. What are you…

JAMES. Then as a friend, I'm asking you – quit with me.

BIEHN. Jimmy – go suit up. Enough with the routine. Your sense of timing is lousy.

JAMES. It's not a routine.

BIEHN. It's not? Well – then, I guess I'll have to suit you up myself. I'll have the team suit you up, how about that?

JAMES. And you can push me out on the field. But I won't say "hike" – I won't hold the ball. I won't pass.

BIEHN. What is wrong with you?

(silence)

You're serious. You're not playing – are you?

JAMES. Yes – I'm serious. I'm not playing.

BIEHN. What did she do to you?

JAMES. It's not her. It's me.

(silence)

BIEHN. Okay – get out of here.

JAMES. But…

BIEHN. Get out of here! *(pause)* Don't start anymore explanations. You told me what you want to do. Fine. I don't need you. We'll win without you. Now go. *(pause)* Goodbye.

*(**JAMES** stands there.)*

BIEHN. Good-bye!

*(**JAMES** moves toward "I", but stops. he moves to "II" and stops. He stands between the two women, not sure where to turn as lights fade to black.)*

ACT II

I (James' Apartment)

(JAMES *and* MADELEINE)

JAMES. She wants to meet you.

MADELEINE. Oh, I'm sure. She gets rid of football, now I'm next.

JAMES. That's not it, at all.

MADELEINE. Of course it is. I'm sure she can't wait to tell me what I did wrong with you.

JAMES. She doesn't think you did anything wrong. She loves me.

MADELEINE. She told you that?

JAMES. No – but...

MADELEINE. But you told her that you...?

(*pause*)

JAMES. Yes.

MADELEINE. When?

JAMES. A week ago.

MADELEINE. Keep it away from me, Jimmy. I don't want to see it.

JAMES. Would you please not worry.

MADELEINE. If you say that to someone and she doesn't say it back – you've scared her. Back-up – fast

JAMES. I don't care if she says it or not.

MADELEINE. *Why* do you love her?

JAMES. She's...she's opened me up.

MADELEINE. "Opened you up?" Please don't talk like some starry-eyed adolescent. You're different.

JAMES. I'm not. The only thing that was different about me was that I wanted to put-down every feeling I had that other people have.

MADELEINE. Well – the armor's off; anything can happen now. Don't tell her you love her anymore. That can get you through a week beautifully. It may even get you through a month, but...

JAMES. Please meet her.

MADELEINE. Okay. Bring her around in about a year.

II (Jan's Apartment)

JAMES. I wonder where we'll be in a year.

JAN. Good question.

JAMES. It's one of those questions that doesn't have an answer – right?

JAN. Right.

JAMES. Well – I have a question that needs an answer.

JAN. What's that?

JAMES. Will you please not do anything with the letters until I can talk to Dick?

JAN. Have you tried to call him?

JAMES. Twelve times. I left messages at his office and with Andrea. I know he's there when I call. I can tell by the way Andrea says he's *not* there. But he...he...I think he hates me.

JAN. And you still call him?

JAMES. You think I shouldn't?

JAN. It's not that. I admire you. If I think someone hates me I tend to stay away. *(pause)* You want me to talk to him?

JAMES. What would you say?

JAN. I don't know really. *(pause)* If we were in an auditorium full of people, I'd know what to say to him. But if I had to see him – alone – face to face… *(pause)* He blames me for everything, doesn't he?

JAMES. He shouldn't.

JAN. But he does.

JAMES. How do you know?

JAN. I've been getting some phone calls from the hard-core fans. As a matter of fact – the phone calls are also hard-core.

JAMES. I'm sorry.

JAN. I don't care. But Jimmy – I don't understand why you're so worried about him – after what he's been doing to you.

JAMES. He only meant to help. I know that. If he knew what he was doing…if he knew about the letters, he'd stop. He just doesn't know. If I showed him the letters, he'd change.

JAN. You're the only one who could almost make me believe that.

(**JAMES** *moves towards her.*)

I've got two papers to type up. So – I'll see you tomorrow?

JAMES. *(pause)* All right.

(He doesn't move.)

JAN. What's wrong?

JAMES. I don't feel right leaving you alone now that I know you're getting those phone calls.

JAN. Oh Jimmy – come on – I'm fine.

JAMES. They threaten you, don't they?

JAN. It's nothing. They're just blowing off steam. They're creeps.

JAMES. Yeah – well – creeps can be dangerous.

JAN. You don't have to worry. I'm a karate expert – I can do doberman pinscher impersonations.

JAMES. I really think I should stay.

JAN. Jimmy – you have things you have to work on too. You have a paper for English – another one for Philosophy...

JAMES. I don't care about that. I could learn more from you in a week, that I could learn in four years of college.

JAN. And I've learned a lot from you. *(pause)* Come over in the morning. We'll have breakfast.

JAMES. All right. I'll bring some bran-muffins

JAN. My favorite.

JAMES. I know. With raisins.

JAN. Has to be with raisins.

JAMES. I'll be home, if you want to call me.

JAN. I'll see you tomorrow.

I (James' Apartment)

*(The phone rings. **JAMES** goes to answer it.)*

MADELEINE. Don't answer it.

JAMES. It might be Coach Biehn

*(**JAMES** answers phone.)*

JAMES. Hello...pardon me? ...No – no. It's not. I don't know where he is...I don't know...I don't know...NO. This is *not* he. I'm sorry – Good-bye.

*(**JAMES** hangs up.)*

MADELEINE. I get twenty of those a day. Lisa usually answers. She loves it. I give her a different story for each call. Her favorite was when I had her tell a sports writer that you were in Poona, India on a retreat. She even gave him a post office box number. But she blew it. She started laughing, so I don't think he bought it.

JAMES. Jan's getting phone-calls too.

> (**MADELEINE** *doesn't respond.*)

They call her names.

> (*pause*)

And they threaten her.

MADELEINE. If she wants – I'll write up some of my stories. She can use them free of charge.

JAMES. They lost yesterday. If they keep losing, it's going to get worse for her.

> (*pause*)

I think she should move in here.

MADELEINE. (*pause*) Have you asked her?

JAMES. Not yet. (*pause*) There's enough room here.

MADELEINE. And you expect me to stay?

JAMES. Yes. Absolutely.

MADELEINE. Jimmy – I don't even want to meet her, and you have the three of us *living* together? Can you imagine what dinners would be like?

JAMES. They could be fun.

MADELEINE. You're maneuvering me out.

JAMES. That's not true.

MADELEINE. Of course it is. You've discovered love-making. Mom and football are out.

JAMES. We haven't made love. The most we've done is kiss – once.

MADELEINE. My God – what is she trying to do to you?

II (Jan's Apartment)

JAMES. Remember when we kissed?

JAN. Yes.

JAMES. That meant an awful lot to me. I know it's ridiculous when people are having affairs with three or four different people at the same time. But that kiss.

JAN. Oh Jimmy. *(He moves toward her.)* Jimmy, I…made a promise to Rich in front of two hundred and thirty-four people. I can't take that lightly. I can't.

I (James' Apartment)

MADELEINE. Is she going to ask for a dispensation from all two hundred thirty-four people? She'll be my age before you can go to bed with her.

JAMES. I admire that. It means I can trust her. I learned some new steps in dance class. Want to see them?

MADELEINE. You're changing the subject.

JAMES. You taught me how to.

(JAMES *dances the steps.*)

JAMES. You want to try it?

MADELEINE. You're wide open for whatever she wants to do.

JAMES. I know. Come on – we'll dance together.

MADELEINE. I guess I can't talk you out of feeling what you're feeling, but please listen to me about your strategy. Forget Lombardi time. Use Bernard time.

JAMES. "Bernard" time?

MADELEINE. That's an hour *after* you're supposed to be there. Give her suspense. Romance *is* suspense. Disappoint her now and then. Bring her bran muffins *without* the raisins.

JAMES. Mom – I can't do that. I don't want to do that.

MADELEINE. You have to, if you want to win.

JAMES. You make it sound like a war.

MADELEINE. It is.

JAMES. Mom, the war is over. Dance.

MADELEINE. It's never over and dancers are the first to go.

III (Neutral Ground)

BIEHN. *(to JAMES)* Hello.

JAMES. Hello. I'm glad you called.

BIEHN. Sorry I didn't call sooner. It just took me a few days to...you know.

JAMES. I've missed you.

BIEHN. Yeah.

JAMES. I want to show you something.

BIEHN. What?

JAMES. Come with me. Let me just show you.

BIEHN. *(pause)* All right.

(They walk towards JAN's apartment.)

JAMES. So – how's Andie?

BIEHN. Good – good. Looking for a job.

JAMES. And Scott?

BIEHN. Getting over a cold.

JAMES. Oh. Well – that'll give him time to draw. Tell him I want another horse. A black one this time.

BIEHN. Where are we going?

JAMES. How's Jeff?

BIEHN. He's starting to grow hair under his arms. He's so happy about it he counts them every morning. They both keep after me about the zoo. They want to know when we're going to take them.

JAMES. "We?" You're coming too?

BIEHN. Yeah.

JAMES. I'll go anytime.

BIEHN. Yeah – you have a lot of free time now – don't you?

(They arrive at JAN's apartment.)

JAMES. Come on in.

BIEHN. *(as he enters)* Whose place is this?

JAN. *(offstage)* Jimmy? Is that you?

(JAN *enters.*)

BIEHN. You've got to be kidding.

JAMES. It's all right. *(to* **JAN***)* He called me back so I thought I'd...

BIEHN. Thought you'd what? Get the two of us together?

JAN. *(to* **BIEHN***)* Uh...please – have a seat...I didn't know Jimmy was going to bring you...

BIEHN. *(to* **JAMES***)* Me neither. What's going on?

JAN. *(to* **BIEHN***)* Can I get you anything to drink?

BIEHN. No. Thanks. *(to* **JAMES***)* What did you want to show me? Her apartment? Is that what you needed to show me?

JAN. You know Jimmy...

BIEHN. Not really. I thought I did.

JAN. ...he likes the people he likes to get along. I've heard a lot about you – from Jimmy. He told me all about your boys - they sound wonderful.

(silence)

I bet it's a real challenge...being a father...nowadays... well – any time really – it's always been a challenge...

(pause)

Are you sure you don't want anything to drink?

BIEHN. Yes. I'm sure.

JAMES. How's the rest of the team? I see some of them in class, but they...they don't talk to me.

BIEHN. Well – you have to understand, Jaimie. They think you're a traitor. They were always behind you – on the field and off. When you were in the hospital, you had more cards and flowers than anyone else on your floor. A day didn't go by without at least ten of the guys visiting you.

JAMES. Now they can visit me at home.

BIEHN. I don't think they will. And poor Pagones. He doesn't like throwing up alone.

JAMES. He should stop putting his hand down his throat.

BIEHN. Yeah – that's funny. *(pause)* Just so you know Jaimie, I get twenty calls a day from sports-writers; the board of directors wants to see me; the alumni association wrote me a five page letter and they all want to know – what happened. They all ask me the same question: "When did he stop loving the game?"

JAMES. I didn't *stop* – I don't think I ever did.

BIEHN. Oh come on. I can't believe that, Jaimie. If you made a touchdown, you danced in the end-zone as much as any other player. More, even.

JAMES. I like to dance. That's probably why I liked making touchdowns – so I could dance.

BIEHN. *(to* **JAN***)* What did you say to him to make him want to quit?

JAMES. It's not anything Jan…

BIEHN. *(to* **JAN***)* I'm just curious. I mean – it's remarkable what you did for your side.

JAN. I'm not part of a team.

BIEHN. *(to* **JAN***)* Neither is Jaimie anymore, and I want to know why. From you. Is he afraid of getting hurt? I know he was worried that everyone seemed to be aiming for his knee. Is that it?

JAMES. I just don't want to get hurt anymore. And I don't want to be glad when someone else gets hurt. The game is not important enough to me anymore to…

BIEHN. It has to be important to you.

JAMES. Why?

BIEHN. Because it's life. Football is life. That's it. Period.

JAN. Whose life?

BIEHN. Anyone's.

JAN. Not mine.

BIEHN. Bullshit.

JAMES. Mr. Biehn – this is her home. It's not right for you….

BIEHN. *(to* **JAN***)* Football is a tough, beautiful game. I mean – here are these men – all from different backgrounds – Blacks, Whites, Hispanics – men who have nothing in common, until they're on this team. And then they organize and work together. Yeah – a few people get hurt but that's how it is. On *this* planet you got to fight. You've got to organize and fight. Didn't you learn history in high-school?

JAN. Not very well. I was too busy learning cheers. Yeah – at sixteen I was a cheerleader. When the score was tight our favorite cheer was, "Blood – Blood – Blood makes the grass grow." I didn't have to learn history. I was being programmed for it.

JAMES. *(to* **BIEHN***)* I didn't want you to come here to fight.

BIEHN. I don't mind. I don't mind fighting for what I want. Everyone does it. *(to* **JAN***)* You do it. It's what you're doing now. But Jaimie – you're a little harder to pin down. You don't fight off the field – you sweat. Why don't you fight? Here she and I are ready to go at each other, and you just sort of watch it happen.

JAN. Actually – he's trying to stop it from happening.

JAMES. I don't know who's right or who's wrong. I just know what I can't do. And I can't play football.

BIEHN. You can. Better than anyone I've ever coached.

JAMES. I didn't ask you here because I want you to change my mind. I wanted you to know that I'm still your friend. I didn't want to cause you any pain. And I wanted to show you…

(He moves to get letters.)

BIEHN. I don't worry about pain – I worry about winning. And we're not going to win without you. You have to come back.

JAMES. I can't.

BIEHN. *(pause)* Please.

*(***JAMES** *moves to embrace* **BIEHN.** **BIEHN** *pushes him away.)*

BIEHN. Don't do that shit. Just tell me to fuck off.

JAMES. I won't.

BIEHN. If what I'm begging you to do is so awful, then I must be some lousy friend. Don't try to hug me – fight me.

JAMES. I won't.

BIEHN. I know what the problem is. I see it real clear now. *(to* **JAMES***)* Your mother has you running in circles because she says she can't walk. *(referring to* **JAN***)* This one tells you football is a "naughty" game, and you quit the team. You have a real problem, Jaimie. The whole team sees it. You were raised by a totally neurotic woman, so now this nit-wit can pull you around by your nose.

JAN. *(to* **BIEHN***)* I think you should go.

JAMES. *(triggered; to* **BIEHN***)* You have girl names for all your players. Is that neurotic? You call me "Jaimie" you call Pagones "Peggy" – Chris Jankowski is "Christine". And you call your wife "Andy" – what's that?

BIEHN. Good Jaimie – good. Show me I can't push you.

JAMES. You made sure we all got gift-grades. What's that?

BIEHN. That's history. No one cares. Come on. More Jaimie. Show her you can fight.

JAMES. You've been having the team doctor shoot me up with painkillers for practically every single game. What's that?

JAN. I think that's enough.

JAMES. No! We have letters from men you've coached. From their doctors.

BIEHN. What letters? What are you talking about?

JAMES. Thirteen men that we know of have permanent injuries, because – as you say – "You don't worry about pain. You worry about winning."

BIEHN. What injuries? You mean Farrell?

JAMES. It's all in the letters, and there are more coming.

BIEHN. *(pause)* What are you going to do with them? *(pause)* You wouldn't do anything with them. You said you're my friend.

JAMES. I wanted to be. But the only reason you called me was because you lost Saturday. I'm only good to you on the field. Well – fine. I'm back on the field. I'll use everything you taught me – only now – you're the opposition!

JAN. Jimmy – stop...

BIEHN. I'll tell you right now – you do anything with those letters, you're in for a fight. You'll be working the rest of your life to pay damages.

JAMES. I am living the rest of my life with damages you caused.

BIEHN. *(to* **JAMES***)* You know me. Backing down is not my style. So if you've decided to do something with them, be ready for big trouble. *(to* **JAN***)* Who says life's not like football? *(to* **JAMES***)* The ball is yours – Jaimie.

I (James' Apartment)

MADELEINE. Drop it.

JAMES. No.

MADELEINE. He was trying to help you.

JAMES. How?

MADELEINE. By stopping the pain.

> (**JAMES** *limps in front of her.*)

JAMES. Look what stopping the pain does, Mom. I'm writing a letter.

II (Jan's Apartment)

JAN. Are you sure you want to?

JAMES. What's the matter? Don't you want me to?

JAN. Yes – but for the right reason.

JAMES. We have to let everyone know he's still doing it. That's important for people to know. Isn't it?

JAN. Just take a night to think about why you're going to write the letter. It probably won't matter to him *why* you do it. But I think eventually it will matter to you.

JAMES. *(pause)* Jan. You're the only one who cares about me.

JAN. Oh, come on Jimmy – things aren't *that* bad.

JAMES. No – they're good. Because you're the only one I need to care about me. You're the only one I want to care about. You don't have to say anything. I know you made a promise. I know you have a lot to figure out. But I wish you'd make a promise to me – I wish you'd live with *me*. We'd find a house – with flower boxes, and a porch, and a hammock. I wish, tomorrow, you'd say you're going to live with me. Don't say anything now. I'll think about what you said. And you think about what I said. And I'll come back tomorrow at 9:00 – in the morning. Okay?

JAN. *(pause)* 9:00? Fine. Fine.

I (James' Apartment)

MADELEINE. You're playing it all wrong.

JAMES. I'm not playing.

MADELEINE. Once she knows you need her, she'll be gone. If you really want her Jimmy – get up off one knee, call her, and take back the proposal.

JAMES. Don't coach me.

MADELEINE. Jimmy…I'm trying to help you with this.

JAMES. I don't want to help. I don't want coaching.

MADELEINE. You need it, whether you want it or not. Let her know you can do without her. Then she'll want you. Those are the facts about people.

JAMES. Those are your facts. I always thought that your facts were the truth. But they aren't

MADELEINE. Oh – really. Well – what are your facts?

JAMES. Let's not talk anymore.

MADELEINE. No. You tell me your facts.

JAMES. You want Jan to say no to me; You don't want her to move in here, because the fact is, you don't want anyone I love near you.

MADELEINE. Believe it or not – I'd rather live with her than live with you after she says no.

JAMES. No! You want me to chase her away with your "facts" the way you chase people away; the way you chased your husband away.

MADELEINE. You were right. Let's not talk anymore. You've proposed to your kissing buddy, you're scared and you're taking it out on me. I won't let you.

JAMES. Then walk away from me.

MADELEINE. Jimmy. Stop it.

JAMES. The fact is – you can walk, but you won't.

MADELEINE. I can't. If no one else believes me, you have to.

JAMES. I have – all along. Just like I believed Coach Biehn and I ended up on an operating table. Mom – the fact is, I had an operation on my knee, and not once have you asked me about it.

MADELEINE. I…I never pitied you – as much as I might have wanted to – I couldn't. I…pity is the worst thing I could ever give you.

JAMES. I don't think that's the reason. You've told yourself that's the reason. But the fact is, you don't really care about my flesh and blood. I'm not a real son to you. I'm your *idea* of a son.

MADELEINE. My God – how long have you been holding that in?

(silence)

I may not have carried you for nine months. But I've carried you since you were four. Everything you felt for all these years, I felt. Every second of your pain was mine; as if you were in me. And that's how I chased my husband away. He couldn't take you and me. He felt left out, so he left – *us*. The fact is, Jimmy – he made me choose – you or him: The same way you're making Jan choose. And if she makes the same mistake I made, don't worry about me. Move her right in – I won't be here.

JAMES. You can't go anywhere.

MADELEINE. Oh yes I can. I'll get better. I will walk. I'll walk just so I can get away from you.

(*JAMES exits to "II".* **MADELEINE** *tries to stand while* **JAMES** *waits for* JAN. JAN *enters.*)

II (Jan's Apartment)

JAMES. Why are you late?

JAN. I'm sorry.

JAMES. We said we'd meet here at nine.

JAN. I wasn't sure of the time.

JAMES. Why not? Where were you?

JAN. (*pause*) He's out.

JAMES. Rich?

JAN. Yes.

JAMES. He called you?

JAN. No. (*pause*) I called him.

JAMES. When?

JAN. Last night.

JAMES. Oh.

(*silence*)

JAN. He's been barred from practicing law for awhile.

JAMES. So what will he do?

JAN. He's going to be a librarian. He worked in the prison library and…

JAMES. Where is he going to be a librarian?

JAN. At a college back east.

JAMES. He must have been happy you called.

JAN. Yes. He was.

JAMES. And he said, he wanted to see you right away; that he's been waiting and waiting for you to call.

JAN. Yes.

JAMES. And you went – right away. *(she nods)* And you're just getting back.

JAN. I told him about you.

JAMES. What did you tell him?

JAN. That you're a hero.

JAMES. So is he. Did you tell him we see each other every day?

JAN. Yes.

JAMES. And he wanted to know if we slept together.

JAN. Yes.

JAMES. And he was glad when you told him we hadn't

JAN. Jimmy...

JAMES. Well – I see you've thought about what I said. And I've thought about the letter – about what I want to put in it. Because I am going to write it. And you know the worst thing the coach did? Something you can't print. He pretended to care. I think people who pretend to care are the cruelest people. They deserve everything they get.

JAN. I didn't pretend to care. Should I have pretended not to care? Would that have been better?

JAMES. So you're leaving. East. Right?

JAN. Yes. East.

JAMES. *(pause)* I'll make it easy for you Jan. You're probably in a hurry. I still have copies of the letters. And I can write my letter by myself, because you've been a wonderful tutor. And I'll take them to the board of directors, get him fired and then I'll make sure they all get printed.

JAN. No Jimmy – I'll do it. You...

JAMES. No – it'll be much more effective coming from an injured party. You're not injured – I am. Everyone will believe it. Every coach that's doing it will think twice about it. I'll go all the way for you Jan. You gave me everything I need to do it with.

JAN. Oh Jimmy –

JAMES. You'll hop from project to project, but you'll never see the person – you'll just see the problem that makes you important. She was right. She's always right.

(JAMES *exits* – JAN *goes to* MADELEINE.)

MADELEINE. *(pause)* Yes?

JAN. Mrs. Bernard – I'm...

MADELEINE. I know who you are.

JAN. I'd like to talk to you.

MADELEINE. Not about Jimmy. I can't

JAN. I'm worried about him.

MADELEINE. I'm trying to remember what I did *before* I worried about him. Now you can take over. Move in.

JAN. I can't. I'm leaving tomorrow.

MADELEINE. Oh. *(pause)* Well – so am I. So he'll have to take care of himself.

JAN. You have to help him.

MADELEINE. You're the tutor. You help him.

JAN. He won't listen to me.

MADELEINE. He hasn't listened to me since he met you. What makes you think he'd listen to me now?

JAN. He said that you're right - you're always right.

MADELEINE. Well – I was right about you. I knew you'd leave.

JAN. I never claimed I wouldn't.

MADELEINE. Does that excuse it? You turn him inside out then you go waltzing back to your husband. But as long as you were careful not to claim you'd never leave Jimmy, "technically" you were fine – is that it?

JAN. No.

MADELEINE. Couldn't you see what would happen? Why didn't you just leave him alone?

III (The Boardroom)

(JAMES *and* BIEHN *before the Board.*)

JAMES. Along with the letters from the alumni, there's also one from me.

BIEHN. You can't take him seriously. He's a very sick kid.

JAMES. He'd explain the injections by saying, "Pain is the enemy, and if we beat pain, we can beat any team."

BIEHN. He has no father. He's looking for one to hate. I played right into it. I made the mistake of treating him like a son.

JAMES. He treated me like a high class call-girl. Gifts, favors, special attention – until I wouldn't put out anymore.

BIEHN. Who talks like this? A stable person?

JAMES. I've gone to the press with all these letters. I suggest you read them as quickly as you can and then get rid of Richard Biehn. I'll make sure the speed of your response is reported. Nothing sells like a good scandal and nothing can hurt a university more. Please know – I mean business.

I (James' Apartment)

JAN. Did you teach him to fight so hard?

MADELEINE. Football taught him. He needed a way to protect himself.

JAN. I'm sure he did –

MADELEINE. He still does. He needs to protect himself from people like you.

JAN. Why? Because I'm leaving? Does that make me the enemy?

MADELEINE. It's how it is.

JAN. I think that's a lie you taught him.

MADELEINE. I never lied to him. Never.

JAN. But once you told him something and he spent all day swinging an axe. Was that a lie?

MADELEINE. *(pause)* He...told you? I...I didn't know he remembered.

JAN. He remembers. And if he keeps believing it, then he'll always have to fight. But he'll never win, he'll never get the tree down. He'll just go in swinging. It'll become a way of life. He's doing it now. He hates me – he hates Coach Biehn – he may even try to hate you. I guess that's the novocaine. I was using it too. It makes you numb for a little while so you *can* fight. But then – like the letters say, the pain comes back worse than ever. When I first saw Jimmy, I was afraid he'd end up a cripple. I still am.

MADELEINE. *(pause)* You mean – like me?

JAN. *Are* you crippled? Jimmy says you can walk?

MADELEINE. Yes – I know. *He* thinks I can dance.

JAN. *(pause)* Why don't you try?

MADELEINE. If he comes home, I'll tell him you were here.

JAN. You know when I knew I loved your son? When he told me why he threw up before each game. It happened to Pagones, so it happened to Jimmy. And I think you're doing the same thing. I think that's why you're not walking. Jimmy got injured – you get injured too. Are you going to sit out the rest of your life, while Jimmy goes in swinging the rest of his? *(pause)* Try to make it better. So he can start to be at peace. You're the only one who can do it. Just – try.

MADELEINE. I'll tell him you were here. That's as much as I can do right now.

JAN. Thank you. *(pause)* Tell him he didn't give me a chance to say good-bye.

(**JAN** *exits.*)

III (Outside Boardroom)

(**JAMES** *and* **BIEHN** *alone.*)

BIEHN. You handled yourself beautifully in there, Jaimie. You weren't intimidated for a second. Just like I taught you. You're a real killer. I'm proud of you.

JAMES. I don't understand you. You act like I did all this to someone else.

BIEHN. In the game – you have to be someone else.

JAMES. I'm not playing a game.

BIEHN. Sure you are, now it's my move. If they fire me, I threaten to sue. And I'll get Chuck Reilly to sue. After all, next to commercials, lawsuits are the best way for ex-players to make money. The guys who wrote those letters may not know that. I wouldn't mind coaching them one more time. And the board of directors will have to decide which they want less: headlines or lawsuits. And then we'll see. It'll be interesting. Oh Jaimie – listen. Do me a favor. Scott and Jeff have been asking for you. Would you give them a call? I wasn't sure what to tell them. You never took them to the zoo. And hey!

(**BIEHN** *puts his arm around* **JAMES.**)

Take care of that knee.

JAMES. *(yelling after him)* I will. And I'll take care of you. I'll fight you all the way. All the way! You won't be here next year – I promise!

I (James' Apartment)

MADELEINE. Jimmy?

(JAMES *moves to "I".*)

I'm leaving tomorrow.

JAMES. Home?

MADELEINE. Yes. *(pause)* Are you all right?

JAMES. I feel great.

MADELEINE. I'm sorry we fought.

(silence)

JAMES. Do you need any help?

MADELEINE. No. I'm all packed. Lisa is going to drive me. She's a good driver. We'll have fun. I love to make her laugh. *(pause)* So you'll be okay?

JAMES. Absolutely. Before – the university gave me everything I wanted because I was a hero. Now they'll give me everything I want because they're afraid of what I'll do next.

MADELEINE. What will you do next?

JAMES. I'm going to settle the score with Coach Biehn, and then I'll be fine. I will. I know just what to do – about everything.

MADELEINE. Yes – I know. Keep everyone at arm's length, and always be ready to do battle, right? Just the way I taught you.

(silence)

Jan came to see me.

(pause)

She wanted to say good-bye to you.

(JAMES *turns away from her. Silence.*)

MADELEINE. She told me you remember our last picnic. I didn't know you did. That's where it began – where you started to be the fighter you are right now. We had such a good time that day – didn't we? We saw a chipmunk, a squirrel – even a deer. And when the day was over, you said – "Where did it go? Where did our good time go?" Remember? And I laughed. And you – you got so mad, because you really wanted to know where that good time was. But I had to laugh. You looked so funny. Your hair was full of leaf-chips – you had acorns in your pockets and flower petals in the cuffs of your pants. *(pause)* And I told you…Jimmy – I told you a lie. You didn't have to chop that tree down. Your hands were all cut and blistered. But I never told you. Jimmy. It's in your hair – it's in the cuffs of your pants – it's in your pockets.

(Silence – he doesn't look at her, although he's heard every word.)

MADELEINE. Jimmy? Before I go – you wanted to dance? Come on.

(After a long pause – he turns to her. She holds out her hands to him. He goes to her. He takes her hands. She leans forward. He helps her as she begins to stand up as…)

(Lights fade.)

www.ingramcontent.com/pod-product-compliance
Lightning Source LLC
Chambersburg PA
CBHW070358120726
47909CB00008B/2908